Pat-a-Cake BABY

illustrated by Polly Dunbar

I'm a cookie baby
a pat-a-cake baby
I want to bake
a very special cake
while everyone is sleeping, but...

THE
KITCHEN'S
WIDE AWAKE.
IT'S WAKING TIME!

So I'm rolling out the bowl
and my spoon is at the ready

for Candy Baby's helping
and Jelly Baby's jumping
and Allsorts Baby's

laughing

'cos they're

oops-a-daisy

bumping.

IT'S BAKING TIME!

With a mutter mutter mutter
pitter patter comes the butter
oh so yellow shiny yellow

And here's the sugar, ditzy sugar,
oh so **GLITZY** oh so **GLOSSY**
and we're frisking while we're whisking 'til it's

flitter flotter

fluffy. **IT'S WHISKING TIME!**

And the eggs say, "Let's get cracking!"

They're yolky and they're jokey

and they're *diving* and they're *smacking*
and they *slither* and they *slide.*

Here's some milk all in a sulk
what's it for for for?
We sip it slop it tip it to make it

pour pour pour.

IT'S POURING TIME!

Now the flour's in a shower
we are sieving shaking sieving
and we're snowy yes we're showy

and it's

all so very blowy.

It's so sweet, oh just so sweet
our spiffy special cake
for a magic midnight treat.

IT'S HULLA-

IT'S HULLA-

BALLOONY-MOON-TIME!

So we've put it in the tin
and the tin into the oven
and we smell it while we cook it
steaming   smelling   sniffing.

We're scraping out the bowl
with an icky flicky licky
and oops we lick each other
and all of us are sticky.

And can you see our cake
RISING RISING RISING
and I've got a funny feeling
it will rise up to the

CEILING, so we've got to jump and catch it ..."

so we can clap and pat it

pit it put it pat it

IT'S PAT

Now we're squeezing and we're piping

icing icing icing

giggle wriggle giggle

and we decorate with silver

squiggle

the cake

balls and jelly diamonds

we
scatter
scatter
hundreds
and
sprinkle
spronkle
thousands.

And our cake is very gooey
chewy yimmy yummy
and we think we're very clever
did you ever ever ever
see a cake that's

just so creamy, so magic moonlight dreamy?

Here's a slice for you

and a slice for me

AND LOOK WHO'S JUST TURNED UP FOR TEA!

IT'S EATING

TIME!

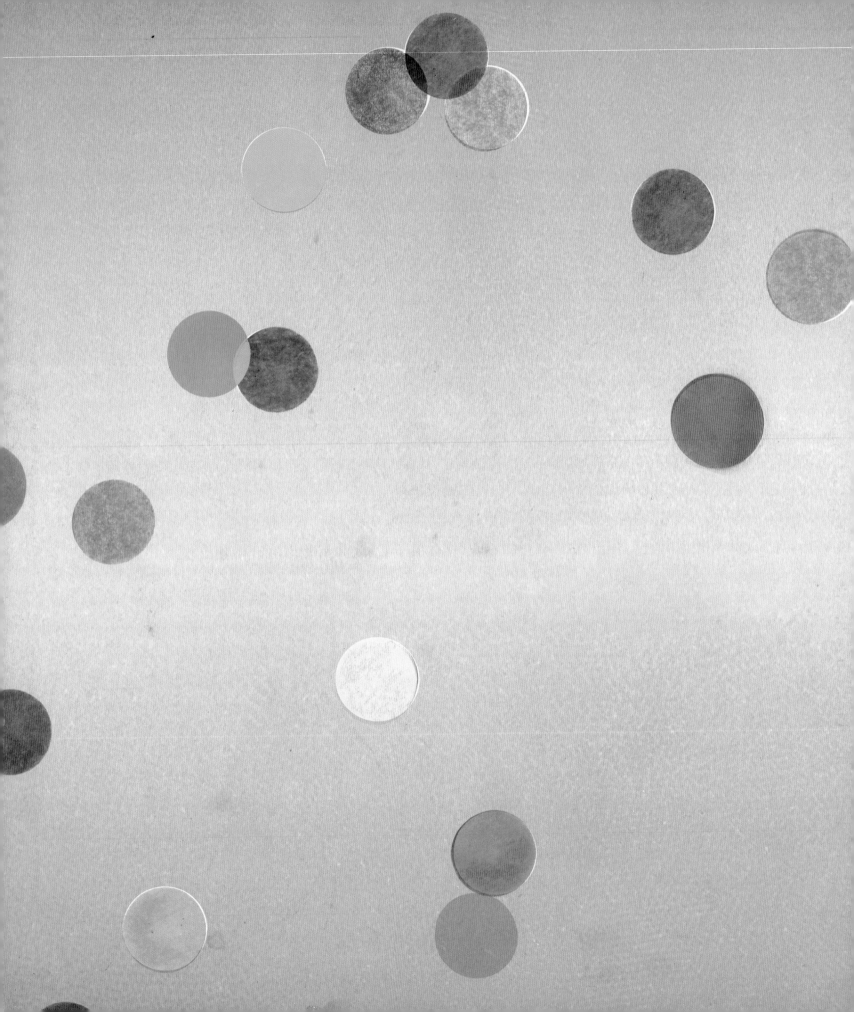